HURRY DOWN TO
DERRY FAIR

For Ann Angel, Sharon Addy, JoAnn Macken, Gretchen Mayo,
and Lisa Moser — in friendship ~ D. C.

For Isaac Jude ~ G. T.

HURRY DOWN TO

DERRY FAIR

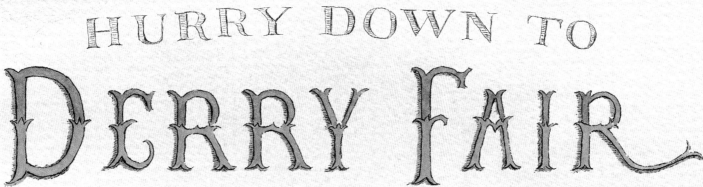

DORI CHACONAS

ILLUSTRATED BY GILLIAN TYLER

CANDLEWICK PRESS

GIANT SWING

"Hurry, Mama! Please, let's go!

Let's go to Derry Fair!

I want to ride the giant swing

That flies high

in the air!"

"Dinny Brown, don't hurry so!
I'm making lemon pies.
I'm going to take them to the fair.
I hope they win a prize!"

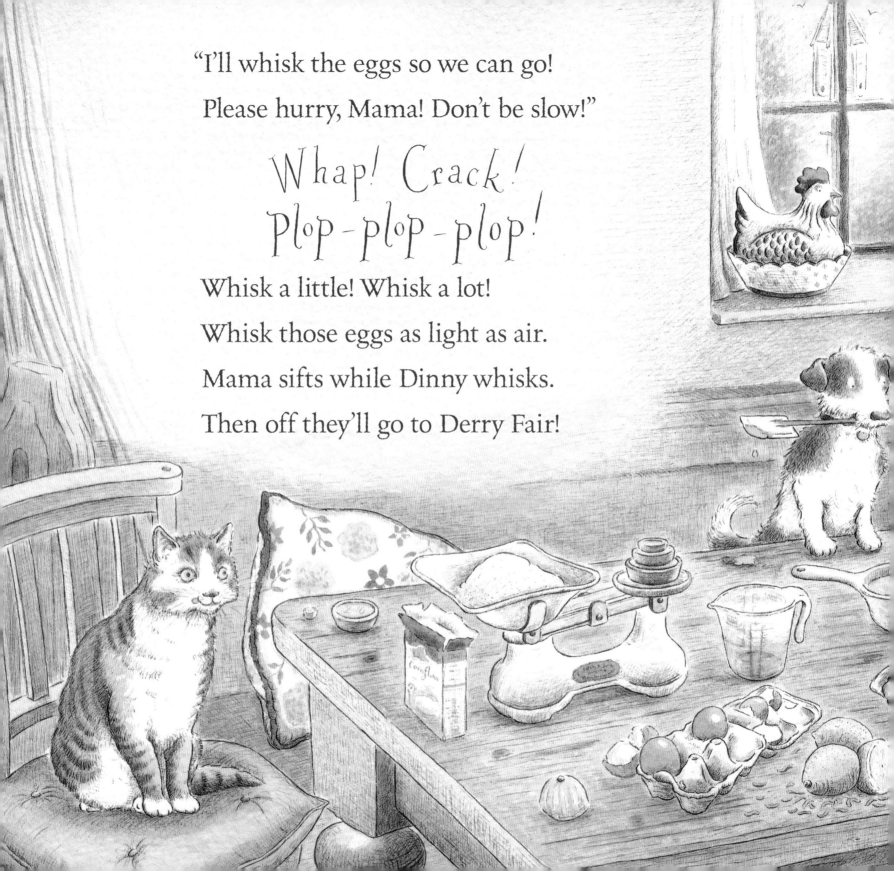

"I'll whisk the eggs so we can go!

Please hurry, Mama! Don't be slow!"

Whap! Crack!
Plop-plop-plop!

Whisk a little! Whisk a lot!

Whisk those eggs as light as air.

Mama sifts while Dinny whisks.

Then off they'll go to Derry Fair!

"Hurry, Daddy! Please! It's time
To walk to Derry Fair.
The rabbits, chickens, woolly sheep,
And horses
     will be there!"

"Dinny Brown, don't worry so!
I need to chop this wood.
I'm going to sell it at the fair.
Please help me
    if you could."

"I'll help you stack so we can go!

Please hurry, Daddy! Don't be slow!"

Whack! smack!
Stack-stack-stack!

Stack a little! Stack a lot!

Wood chips in a flying flurry.

Whack 'em, smack 'em, stack 'em high!

Almost finished!

Hurry! Hurry!

"Sister Lucy, time to go!

If we don't get there soon,

We'll miss the cotton candy

And the red

hot-air balloon!"

"Dinny Brown, don't worry so!

My animals need brushing.

I'm going to show them at the fair.

Please help me!

Stop your rushing!"

"Lucy, you are much too slow!
We're going to miss the talent show!"

Swish! Swash!
Swoosh – swoosh – swoosh!

Brush a little! Brush a lot!
Piggy, puppy, old gray goosey.
Fur and feathers fly about
While Dinny hurries Sister Lucy.

"Grandma Patty! Time to go!

The Derry Fair won't wait!

We're going to miss the Ferris wheel!"

"You're right," she said.
"It's late!"

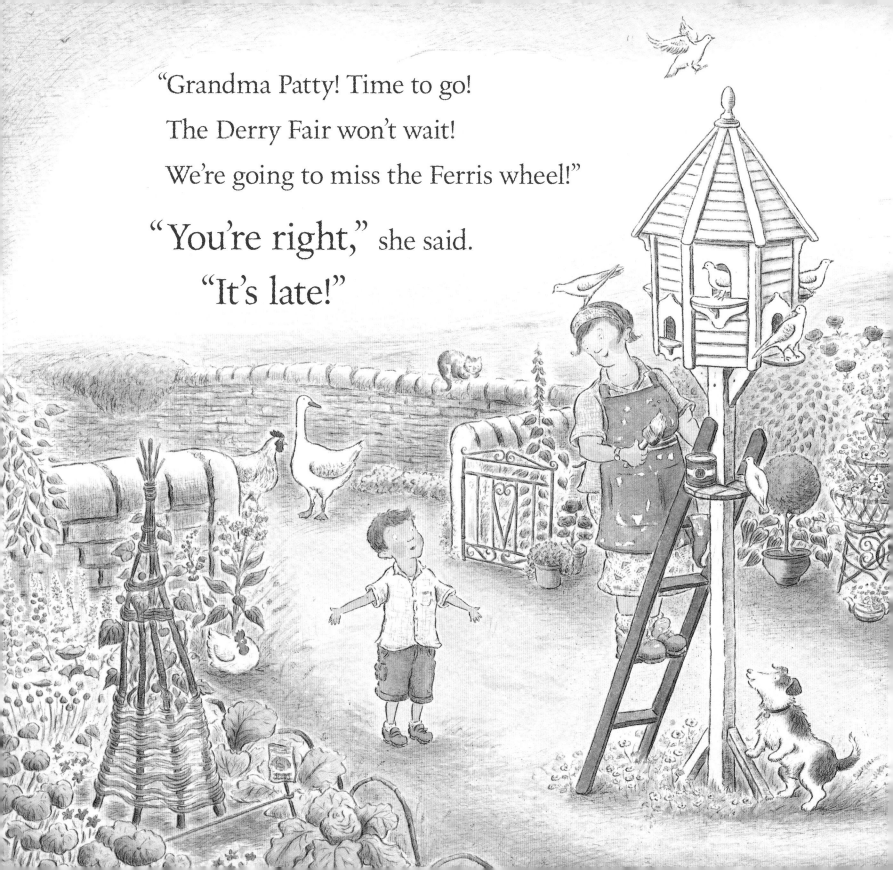

"So Dinny Brown,

      go fetch your coins,

Then meet me at the door.

I'm taking you to Derry Fair!

You won't wait anymore!"

"We're leaving now!" calls Grandma Patty.

"See you later, Mama, Daddy!

Sister Lucy, you take care!"

Mama bundles up the pies
And slips them in a sack.

Daddy bundles up the wood
And slings it on his back.

Lucy bundles up her pets
And hurries to the gate.

They rush and tumble
down the walk.

Dinny,
Grandma—
Wait!

Mama, Daddy, Sister Lucy,

Grandma, piggy, puppy, goosey,

Running down the road to town

To see the fair with Dinny Brown!

HORTICULTURE

Library of Congress Catalog Card Number pending   ISBN 978-0-7636-3208-3   Printed in Heshan, Guangdong, China.
This book was typeset in Quercus. The illustrations were done in watercolor and ink. Candlewick Press, 99 Dover Street,
Somerville, Massachusetts 02144. visit us at www.candlewick.com. 11 12 13 14 15 16 LEO 10 9 8 7 6 5 4 3 2 1